120525

MYTHS
OF THE
ORIENT
by
Barbara Christesen

A
(cpi)
Book

From

RAINTREE CHILDRENS BOOKS
Milwaukee • Toronto • Melbourne • London

Library of Congress Number: 77-22199

Art and Photo Credits

**Cover illustration and illustrations on pages 8, 9, 11, 14, 15, 18, 21, 27, 29, 32, 35,
37, 38, 44, 45, and 47 by Wayne Atkinson**
Photo on page 43, The United Nations
Every effort has been made to trace the ownership of all copyrighted material in
this book and to obtain permission for its use.

Library of Congress Cataloging in Publication Data

Christesen, Barbara, 1940-
Myths of the Orient.

CONTENTS: The ugliest god.—The faithful son and the weaving
goddess.—The magic gourd.—The bell of many metals. [etc.]
1. Tales, Chinese. [1. Folklore—China] I. Title.
PZ8.1.C4624My   398.2'0951   77-22199
ISBN 0-8172-1043-1 lib. bdg.

Manufactured in the United States of America
ISBN 0-8172-1043-1

Contents

Introduction

Some of the most magical myths of the ages began in the old world of China. These wonderful stories reach us from the ancient past. They have been passed for centuries from father and mother to daughter and son.

We have written down some of the myths that describe the magical deeds of the many Chinese gods who helped the good and punished the evil. If you can't believe these ancient Chinese "tall tales," can you at least believe that the people who told them didn't really believe them either? Perhaps the Chinese tellers of tales had something else in mind when they repeated these myths. What do you think?

5

Chapter 1

The Ugliest God

Did you know that there was once a Chinese god who helped students pass their tests? Well there was—at least there is an old Chinese tale that says there was. There were two things about this god that made him different from the other Chinese gods. He began his life as a human, and he had a very ugly face. Here is the story of how he became a god.

Once there was a boy named *K'uei*. He was brilliant and spent all his time studying. He never rested or played games with the other boys. Oh, he would have liked to join them, but other children would have nothing to do with him. You see, poor K'uei was so horrible looking that no one could bear to look at his face.

So K'uei buried himself among his books. They were the only friends he had ever known. He studied his books until he knew them all by heart. As he grew to manhood he became known far and wide as one of the smartest men in all China. But K'uei was never seen in the company of another human being. Even the kindest people had to turn from his poor ugly face.

Once a year the Emperor of China held a contest. He would give a golden rose to the boy or girl with the highest marks in the national examinations. When K'uei was 20 years old, he entered this contest and easily won the highest honors. The night before the awards ceremony, K'uei was so excited he could not sleep a wink. The very thought of being presented to the Emperor filled him with a joy unlike anything he had ever known.

The next morning K'uei dressed himself in his best robe and hurried to the palace. He waited breathlessly until his name was called. Then he proudly walked to the throne of the Emperor and bowed his most humble bow. But when K'uei raised his head and showed his ugly face, the Emperor was horrified. He was so shocked that the golden rose fell and broke into a thousand pieces.

The golden rose broke into a thousand pieces.

K'uei had known many insults in his life, but this was the final disgrace. The poor young man ran from the palace. He ran all the way to the sea and tried to drown himself. But just as the water was about to close over K'uei for the last time, a strange thing happened. A sea monster swam under him and lifted him up above the water.

The monster broke through the waves and, with K'uei still on its back, began to climb higher and higher into the sky. Finally, they

8

reached the heavenly home of the Chinese gods. There no one shuddered at the sight of K'uei's ugliness. The gods welcomed him, praised him for his brilliance, and told him that this would be his new home.

K'uei was given a golden throne among the stars of the Big Dipper. The people on earth could look up at him and say, "How beautiful he is!" The young man with the hideous face was raised to the rank of a god. He was worshipped by the very people who had once teased him for his ugliness.

With K'uei on its back, the monster climbed higher and higher.

Chapter 2

The Faithful Son and the Weaving Goddess

Sometimes the gods and goddesses left their heavenly homes and came to earth. They often made the trip to reward someone for some special good deed. Such a person was *Tung Yung*. He showed great respect for the dead.

Tung Yung lived with his old father. They were so poor that they had barely enough rice to eat each day. When the old man died, the young boy was very frightened. He had no money to give his father a funeral.

Everyone knew that the soul of a dead person could never find its way to Heaven without a proper funeral. A tomb had to be built. Regular offerings to the gods had to be made. Tung

How could Tung Yung give his father a proper funeral?

Yung was beside himself with grief. "What kind of son am I," he cried, "to let the soul of my beloved father wander through the mists, never to find rest?"

Tung Yung looked about his poor hut. He saw nothing he could sell to raise money for his father's funeral. But he knew that wealthy landowners would often use young men as slaves in their fields. Tung Yung knew what he had to do. He would sell himself as a slave.

The very next morning, Tung Yung went to the slave market. He offered himself for sale at

a very high price. He caught the eye of a nobleman who willingly paid the price that the boy
demanded. Tung Yung knew that he would have
to work until the nobleman had received his
money's worth. That might be forever. But it
didn't matter.

He used the nobleman's money to give his
father a proper funeral. He was able to have a
small tomb built in a peaceful, shaded wood.
Tung Yung then presented himself to his new
master to begin his life of slavery. But his mind
was at peace, for each evening he could visit the
tomb of his father.

From dawn to sunset, Tung Yung worked in
the rice fields. Years passed. The young man's
body was growing old. He ached all over from
the years of back-breaking work. Even worse
than the aching was the great sadness he felt.
There was no one left to share his life with him.
At last his strength gave out, and he was over-
come with fever.

His fellow slaves carried Tung Yung to his
hut and left him there. No one could stop work-
ing to care for the sick man. Tung Yung lay alone
in the dark, little hut. There was no one to cook
his meals or bring him water to quench his burn-
ing thirst. Tung Yung was at the point of death.

But the mightiest god looked down from his starry throne and took pity on the dying man. He knew Tung Yung had shown great devotion to his dying father. The greatest god sent for his daughter, *Tchi-Niu,* the beautiful *goddess of weaving,* and spoke this to her:

"My daughter, I must ask you to leave our heavenly home for a while. I have a job for you to do on earth. Go to the dying Tung Yung. Care for him. Be his wife. This young man's respect for his dead father cannot go unrewarded. You, my beloved, must bring joy to his empty life."

Tchi-Niu did as her father commanded. As Tung Yung lay asleep, he dreamed that a soft, cool hand was touching his fevered brow. At the touch, the pain in his body seemed to melt away. The young man opened his eyes, and there beside his bed was a lovely maiden. Her skin was pale and smooth as ivory. Peach blossoms perfumed her glossy black hair. He thought that he still must be dreaming.

The girl brought him fresh rice cakes and tea. *Now he knew this was no dream.* He was about to ask her who she was, but she silenced him with a smile. "Do not be troubled," she said. "I have come from far away to be your wife.

From this day on, you will never know loneliness again."

Tung Yung had never been so happy! He returned to work. The days in the fields now seemed to pass quickly. After all, Tung Yung had a beautiful, loving wife and a comfortable home waiting for him.

All day long, while Tung Yung worked in the fields, Tchi-Niu sat at her loom weaving beautiful, silk cloth. Her fingers fairly flew across the

While Tung Yung worked in the fields, Tchi-Niu wove silk cloth.

Tchi-Niu surprised Tung Yung with an important piece of paper.

loom. Beautiful cloth flowed in folds of brilliant red, jade green, and gold as bright as the sun itself. The fame of Tchi-Niu's weaving spread far and wide. People from all over the kingdom came to buy her fairy-like silk cloth.

One day, as Tung Yung was returning from the fields, Tchi-Niu ran to meet him. In her hands was a piece of paper bearing the seal of Tung Yung's master. Imagine the young man's joy when he read his official notice of freedom!

15

His faithful wife, Tchi-Niu, had paid her husband's debts with the pieces of silver she had received for her silks.

But Tung Yung's happiness was just beginning. His wife had also bought him a large home and fields of his own. And it was not long thereafter that a son was born to the young couple. Tung Yung now had everything he could ask for. He had wealth, comfort, and a child to care for him the way he had cared for his father.

Chapter 3

The Magic Bottle

The *Eight Immortals* were persons who were rewarded by the gods for goodness and wisdom. The eight were given the gift of godliness. The Chinese believed these new gods roamed the world in search of adventure. They often disguised themselves as ordinary humans. The Eight Immortals were pictured on many old vases and weavings. One of them was always shown carrying a wooden bottle. Knowing this story of the Eight Immortals will help as you read the following tale of old China.

One day, in a crowded Chinese city, a new peddler began to sell medicines in the city

17

The new peddler sat mysteriously in the city square.

square. The old man spread out his herbs, and pills, and powders, and syrups in an attractive display. Few people could resist buying them.

Business was so good that he came to the square every morning. The peddler would sit on a little wooden stool from early morning until the last rays of the sun had disappeared. No one knew his name, for he did not care to tell it. Since he always hung a wooden bottle on the

wall near his stool, he was soon given the nick-
name *Hu Kung—the old man of the wooden
bottle.*

Every day crowds of shoppers came and
went. Hu Kung did well selling his herbs and
powders. No one bothered to ask the old man
any questions. But there was one young man,
Wong Fei, who became curious. Wong Fei lived
in an old house across from the square. Watch-
ing Hu Kung each day, he wondered where the
old man went when he left the square at night.
Did he live by himself in some miserable hut?
Was there anyone to care for him?

One night Wong Fei sat by his window and
watched carefully as the old man began to pack
up his medicines. He saw the old man look
about him in every direction to make sure that
he was quite alone. Then he clapped his hands,
and before the disbelieving eyes of Wong Fei,
the old man jumped into the wooden bottle!

At first Wong Fei hoped he was dreaming.
But he knew this was no dream. He had seen the
marvelous happening with his own eyes. Surely
this old medicine-seller was no ordinary human.
Hu Kung seemed to know the magic of the gods
themselves.

The very next day, Wong Fei went to the medicine-seller's stand. He bought some dried herbs. As he paid Hu Kung for the medicine, he began a conversation with the old man.

"Good sir," said Wong Fei, "you must get thirsty, sitting here all day in the hot sun. I should like you to come across the street to my house and join me for tea."

"That is most kind of you," said the old man. "I would be happy to come."

And so Wong Fei and the old medicine-seller became friends. Each afternoon they would sit together and sip tea in the coolness of Wong Fei's modest home. At last the young man called together all his courage and said to Hu Kung, "Honorable sir, I would consider it a great honor to be invited to your home one evening."

The old man thought for a moment. Then he answered, "You have been very kind to me, and I will repay your kindness. Meet me in the square tonight."

Wong Fei could hardly wait. Every nerve in his body thrilled with excitement. He hurried to meet the old man at sunset. He found Hu Kung

Wong Fei could not believe the riches in the wooden bottle.

packing his medicines away. The old man
greeted Wong Fei. Then he looked around to
make sure no one else was in the street. Pointing
to the wooden bottle that hung on the wall, he
said to Wong Fei, "Come with me."

Then he clapped his hands, and in the very
twinkling of an eye the two men were inside the
bottle. And what a sight greeted the eyes of
Wong Fei! For he found himself in a mansion
more beautiful than that of the mightiest emperor. The richness of its furnishings and won-

21

derful works of art left Wong Fei unable to speak. Never in all his dreams could he have imagined so wonderful a home.

As he stood there, the medicine-seller invited him to sit at a table on which a great feast had been set. The two sat down and dined on the choicest of meats, the most delicate of fish, the rarest of fruits and cakes. As they ate, they drank wine so sweet and powerful that it made Wong Fei's head swim. Wong Fei became drowsy from the wine and soon fell into a deep sleep.

He awoke the next morning with an aching head. Slowly, he sat up and looked around him. *He was in his own bed.* Wong Fei held his head and tried to think clearly. Had it all been a dream? Wong Fei threw on his clothes and ran outside to the street to find the old medicine-seller.

But the stand where Hu Kung had once sold his medicines was empty. The wooden bottle no longer hung on the wall. Hu Kung had disappeared as mysteriously as he had first appeared. Wong Fei would never know what had happened to him during that one magical night. He would never know who that old man really was. Do you?

Chapter 4

The Bell
of Many Metals

Many centuries ago, the Emperor *Ming Yong-lo* ruled China from his palace in the Imperial City of Peking. This mighty ruler had a tall, stone tower built high above the city. He ordered that a bell of great size and tone be hung in the tower. Its ringing would reach every corner of Peking.

From the four corners of the empire, bell-makers were called in to do the great work. They gathered before the master bellmaker, *Kwan Yu*, and listened carefully as he read the orders the Emperor had given.

"The sound of this bell must be unlike any bell ever heard in China," read Kwan Yu. "Its *iron* must be mixed with *brass* to make its voice strong. *Gold* must be added to make its tone rich. It must have *silver* to give its song sweetness. Of these four metals must the bell be cast."

The bellmakers knew the Emperor's orders would be hard to carry out. They worked night and day. They built a great mold, larger than any ever seen. Iron, brass, gold, and silver were brought to Peking from far-off mines. Each was melted to a boiling liquid. In a huge pot the four boiling metals were mixed together. At last, the mixture was ready to be poured into the mold.

The Emperor and his entire court came to watch the casting of the bell. Kwan Yu gave the order, and the white-hot liquid metal was poured into the bell mold. Kwan Yu was left alone to wait for the mold to cool. So great was its size that the cooling took many days. Finally, Kwan Yu decided the hour had arrived for the bell to be removed from the mold. He sent for his assistants, and the great work was done.

Alas! The sight of the new bell brought no joy to their hearts. The gold, silver, brass, and iron had refused to mix with one another. Instead of having a smooth, polished surface, the bell was filled with cracks and spaces, like the webs of giant spiders.

When the news reached the Emperor, he was very angry. He gave orders for the bell to be recast immediately. Kwan Yu went to work immediately on the second bell. When the time came to remove the bell from the mold, the Emperor himself was present. Kwan Yu held his breath as the great bell was lifted from the mold. The sight of the bell brought a cry of dismay from all present.

This second bell looked even worse than the first. Great holes marred its sides, and its shining edges were cracked and split. Even more stubbornly than before, the four metals would not mix with one another.

The Emperor was beside himself with fury. He spoke to the master bellmaker in a voice that shook with rage. "Kwan Yu, twice I placed my trust in you. Twice you have failed me. In my great mercy I will give you one more chance. But should you fail a third time, your head will be quickly removed from your neck. Hear the words of your Emperor, and see to your job at once!"

The trembling bellmaker did not know that his daughter, *Ko Ngai*, was standing nearby. She heard the Emperor's words and she trembled with fear. The young girl loved her father more than life itself. All day long, Ko Ngai sat and wept, trying to think of some way that she could help her father.

Kwan Yu wearily began once more to prepare the metals and the fires and the mold. He would cast the bell a *third* time! But his heart was filled with sadness. "These four metals will not blend with one another," he cried. "It is hopeless. I am a doomed man."

While the bellmaker worked, Ko Ngai secretly slipped away to the hut of the local fortune-teller. She told the wise man of the problem. He thought a long time before he gave his advice. The young girl waited nervously, until she thought she could wait no more. Finally, in a low voice, he told her what the gods had said to him.

"My child, your father will surely lose his life. Gold will never mix with iron. Brass and silver will never blend. The bell will never be made, unless the flesh and blood of a young girl

Ko Ngai trembled when she heard the Emperor's words.

27

are mixed with the melted metals before they are cast. I am sorry."

Ko Ngai bowed her head, thanked the fortune-teller, and sadly returned home. She told no one where she had been. The day drew near for the bell to be cast once again. Ko Ngai asked her father if she might go with him to watch. Kwan Yu could not refuse his beloved daughter.

At the appointed hour, Ko Ngai and her old nurse stood on the platform above the huge melting-pot and the bubbling metals. The Emperor was there too, a grave look on his face. At his side was the Royal Executioner, his terrible axe in his hand.

Trembling, Kwan Yu gave the signal for the bell to be cast. But a sudden movement on the platform caused the workers to freeze in their tracks. Ko Ngai rushed forward and was climbing over the wooden railing. Her old nurse tried to catch hold of her foot, but the girl's shoe came off in her hand. "My life for yours, my beloved father," cried Ko Ngai, and in an instant she plunged into the white-hot mass of liquid metal below.

The metal rose up like a fountain to receive her, and then all was still. Not a trace could be seen of the girl's body. On the platform above, workers had to hold Kwan Yu to keep him from following his daughter. The old nurse sobbed and rocked back and forth, still holding the shoe in her hand.

In spite of all this grief, the Emperor's orders had to be carried out. The bell was cast, allowed to cool, and removed from the mold. *It*

"My life for yours, my beloved father," cried Ko Ngai.

29

was perfect! The color and the form were more beautiful than any bell ever seen. And the tone of the bell! When it was hung in the great tower and rung, people all over Peking were *enchanted.*

But the most striking feature of the bell was a certain sound it made that no one had ever heard from a bell before. Each time it was struck, its golden tone was followed by a long, whispering sigh. For many hundreds of years, whenever the people of Peking heard that sigh, they would say that Ko Ngai was calling for her lost shoe.

Chapter 5

Ming Li
and the Tortoise

In a small village near the Yellow River, there once lived a young man named *Ming Li*. He was not rich in worldly goods, but he had a kind and generous heart. He could not harm any living creature.

One day a fisherman from the village came to Ming Li's hut carrying a large tortoise which he had just caught. The fisherman had borrowed money from Ming Li and wished to repay his debt. "This tortoise will feed you for many days," said the fisherman. "Forgive me, Ming Li, but it is all I have to give you."

Ming Li had never seen such a beautiful and unusual tortoise.

Ming Li bowed and graciously thanked the fisherman. When he was alone, he looked closely at the beautiful and unusual tortoise. On its forehead there was a strange white mark. It looked like a very special symbol. But Ming Li did not know its meaning. He pitied the poor creature. "I cannot eat you, you beautiful tortoise," he said sadly. With great difficulty he carried the heavy tortoise down to the river and set it free.

A few weeks later, Ming Li was on his way home from a neighboring village. Suddenly, he saw a royal parade coming toward him. In a covered chair carried by four servants sat a proud young prince. His robes were of the richest silk and his hands were covered with jeweled rings.

"You there!" the prince called to Ming Li. "Get out of my way and let me pass. Be quick about it!"

Ming Li did not like the prince's manner. But he controlled his anger. "Good sir," he replied, "I am not one of your servants. I have as much right to walk on this path as you."

The prince was furious. He ordered his servants to take hold of Ming Li and give him a good beating. At that, Ming Li could no longer hold back his anger. "You may be of royal blood," he cried, "but you know nothing of the ways of kindness and good manners. My name is Ming Li. I am on my way home, and I do no man any harm. You have no right to treat me like one of your slaves."

At the very mention of Ming Li's name, a sudden change came over the prince. He climbed down from his great chair and bowed low before the young man. "Please forgive me, Ming Li," he said in the humblest of tones. "It is you who saved my life; I am forever in your debt."

Now Ming Li did not understand why the prince spoke these words. As he stood there, confused, the prince rose from his knees and begged Ming Li to go with him to his home. "I must try to repay your great kindness," said the prince.

The puzzled Ming Li sat down next to the prince in the covered chair. The servants carried the two men to the prince's palace. Ming Li was led to a low table carved of the most precious teakwood and covered with jade. The servants brought in a delicious dinner. Never had Ming Li dreamed of tasting food such as he was served that day.

Afterward, as the two men were sipping tea, a bell suddenly rang some distance away. It seemed to scare the prince, and he quickly rose to his feet. "I pray you, excuse me," he said politely. "I must go now. But first, I would like to give you a gift that you may keep for a while. It will make all your wishes come true."

Without warning, the prince seized Ming Li's arm in a powerful grip. He pinched Ming Li's skin so hard that the pain brought tears to the young man's eyes. Ming Li was stunned. Why was the prince treating him this way? But before he could ask, the prince led him to the door and bowed good-bye.

The painful pinch left a mark on Ming Li's arm.

Still stunned, Ming Li began to walk slowly from the prince's mansion. His arm stung, and he stared at the spot where the prince had pinched him. Ming Li stopped short in amazement. There on his arm was the outline of a tortoise with a white mark on its head!

Ming Li's head began to spin as he tried to understand all that had happened. But the greatest wonders were yet to come. For as Ming Li stared at the ground, he suddenly realized that he could see right through it. About a foot below the surface, he could see a huge pearl.

Ming Li dug it from the earth and carried the pearl home. He soon discovered that wherever he looked, he could see jewels and precious stones lying deep in the earth. By the time he reached his poor hut, he carried enough treasures to make him the richest man in all the countryside.

Word of Ming Li's great wealth reached the ears of the son of the Emperor himself. He sent for Ming Li and offered him his daughter's hand in marriage. The girl was a lovely creature with a kind heart and smiling ways. Ming Li could not refuse. A royal wedding took place, followed by weeks of feasting and ceremony. Then Ming Li

Ming Li suddenly realized he could see right through the ground!

brought his new wife home to his own new palace.

One night not long afterward, Ming Li sat alone in his drawing room. He heard a noise at the door and looked up. There stood the prince. "I do not have much time, Ming Li," said the prince with a smile. "I know that you are happy and that all your heart's wishes have been answered. It is time for me to take back the gift I gave you. You no longer need it."

The prince seized Ming Li's arm as before and pinched it with all his strength. Tears of pain blinded Ming Li for a few seconds. When he opened his eyes once more, the prince was

In the darkness, Ming Li could see the mysterious tortoise.

gone. He looked at his arm and saw that the mark of the tortoise had disappeared.

Ming Li could not let the prince leave without thanking him for the happy life he had given a poor young man. He rushed to the door. He ran outside and looked everywhere, but he could not find the prince. Ming Li peered through the mist along the river bank. Not too far from him, at the edge of the water, he saw the only other living creature for miles. It was a large tortoise with a white mark on its forehead. The tortoise jumped into the river, never to be seen again.

Chapter 6

The Story of Wan and his Faithful Wife

More than 2,000 years ago, a cruel Emperor named *Chin Shih Huang Ti* sat on the Dragon Throne of China. The people lived in fear of the hated Emperor. The Emperor, too, was fearful —not of the people, but of attacks by tribes from the north. These invaders often crossed the border of China on horseback. They burned Chinese villages and towns.

The cruel Emperor thought of a brilliant plan to keep his enemies out. He would have a Great Wall built across the entire northern boundary of China. It would stretch from the sea to the mountains of Tibet—*a distance of 1,500 miles.*

The people thought that Chin Shih Huang Ti had truly gone mad. More than one-third of the men in China were dragged from their homes and forced to work at building the Wall. Even old men and women had to carry huge stones and heavy bricks for the Wall. Farmers had to supply most of their food to the workers at the Wall. Everyone else in China had to starve.

The poor workers were whipped and treated so cruelly that more than half a million of them died building the Wall. Their bodies were never buried. They were merely thrown among the bricks and stones. Any worker who left even the tiniest crack in the Wall was beheaded.

According to one legend, the heads of the workers began to look green. This was because the men slaved so long at the Wall that grass grew out of the dust that filled their hair.

Down through the ages, many tales have been told about the Great Wall of China. One of the most famous stories tells how the Emperor sent for a fortune-teller to give him advice about the building of the Wall.

The fortune-teller did not have good news for the Emperor. He told him that the Wall would never be completed unless 10,000 young men were buried alive in it as a sacrifice to the gods.

Now the Emperor did not like the idea of killing so many valuable workers. He came up with a better idea. He would find a man named *Wan*, which means "ten thousand," and have him buried in the Wall. In this way the gods would be satisfied, and the rest of the young men in China could go on building the Great Wall.

The Emperor sent his soldiers throughout the land to search for a young man named Wan. At last, they found one. Wan came from a fine family and had just been married. The Emperor's soldiers broke into his home and dragged him away from his bride, the beautiful *Meng Chiang*. The soldiers told the young wife that her husband was being taken to work at the Wall and that he would return to her in a few months.

Many tales have been told about the Great Wall of China.

Months passed, and there was no word from Wan. Meng couldn't stand the waiting. She decided to go and search for her husband. It was many hundreds of miles to the Great Wall, and winter was approaching. But the brave, young wife set out on foot to make the journey.

Finally, after traveling for six months, she reached the Great Wall. It loomed before her, gray and gloomy. Meng Chiang asked everyone she met if they knew the whereabouts of her husband Wan. At last someone told her that Wan had been buried inside the Wall as a sacrifice to the gods.

Meng Chiang's tears washed away the stones in the Wall.

Meng Chiang began to weep, and never before had such weeping been heard in all of China. Tears flowed from her eyes in such great streams that they flooded the Wall, washing away some of the stones. A great section of the Wall collapsed. There, among the ruins, lay the bones of hundreds of men who had died building the Wall.

Meng Chiang called upon the gods to help her find the remains of her husband. She cut her wrist and prayed that her blood might be united with the bones of her husband. The blood from Meng's wrist flowed along the ground for a short distance. The blood stopped near a pile of bones among the ruins of the Wall. The blood seeped into these bones, turning them bright red.

Among the ruins lay the bones of hundreds of men.

45

Meng ran to the spot. She realized that she had found her dead husband and she fainted.

Guards at the Wall had seen these miracles and sent word to the Emperor. When the Emperor heard of Meng's great courage and the wonderful things that she had done, he had her brought to him. Seeing Meng's great beauty, he made up his mind at once to marry her.

Meng Chiang said that she would become the Emperor's wife, if he would agree to three things. The Emperor promised to grant her every wish. Then Meng asked the Emperor to declare a two-month period of mourning for her husband. Second, she asked that a great tomb be built on the side of the Wall that faced the sea. Her last request was that all the Emperor's ministers and high officials must attend the funeral service.

The mourning period was observed as Meng had asked. When it was over, arrangements were made for the funeral service. At the appointed hour, the Emperor and his court sat before the new tomb that had been built on top of the Wall. Suddenly, the young widow rose and faced the Emperor, her face twisted in hatred. In a loud voice that could be heard by everyone there, she cried out:

46

Meng leaped into the freezing water.

"Chin Shih Huang Ti! You are the cruelest tyrant ever to rule China. You have made your people suffer. You have taken everything from them. May you and your children be cursed forever!"

And then, before anyone could make a move to stop her, Meng turned toward the sea and leaped into the freezing water.

47

As the people on the Wall looked down at Meng's body floating on the waves, they saw it change slowly into a great, silver fish. It is said that this silver fish still swims in the sea near the edge of the Great Wall of China.